USBORNE
Puzzle Adventures
The Dark Dark Knight

Lesley Sims
Illustrated by Peter Wingham

Contents

- 2 The prophecy
- 6 Carved in stone
- 10 Hamalot's Burger Bar
- 12 The quest
- 18 Books and clues
- 22 Arabian knights
- 28 Herman the Hermit
- 30 The labyrinth
- 36 Inside the tower
- 40 The last battle of all
- 42 A dark knight ends

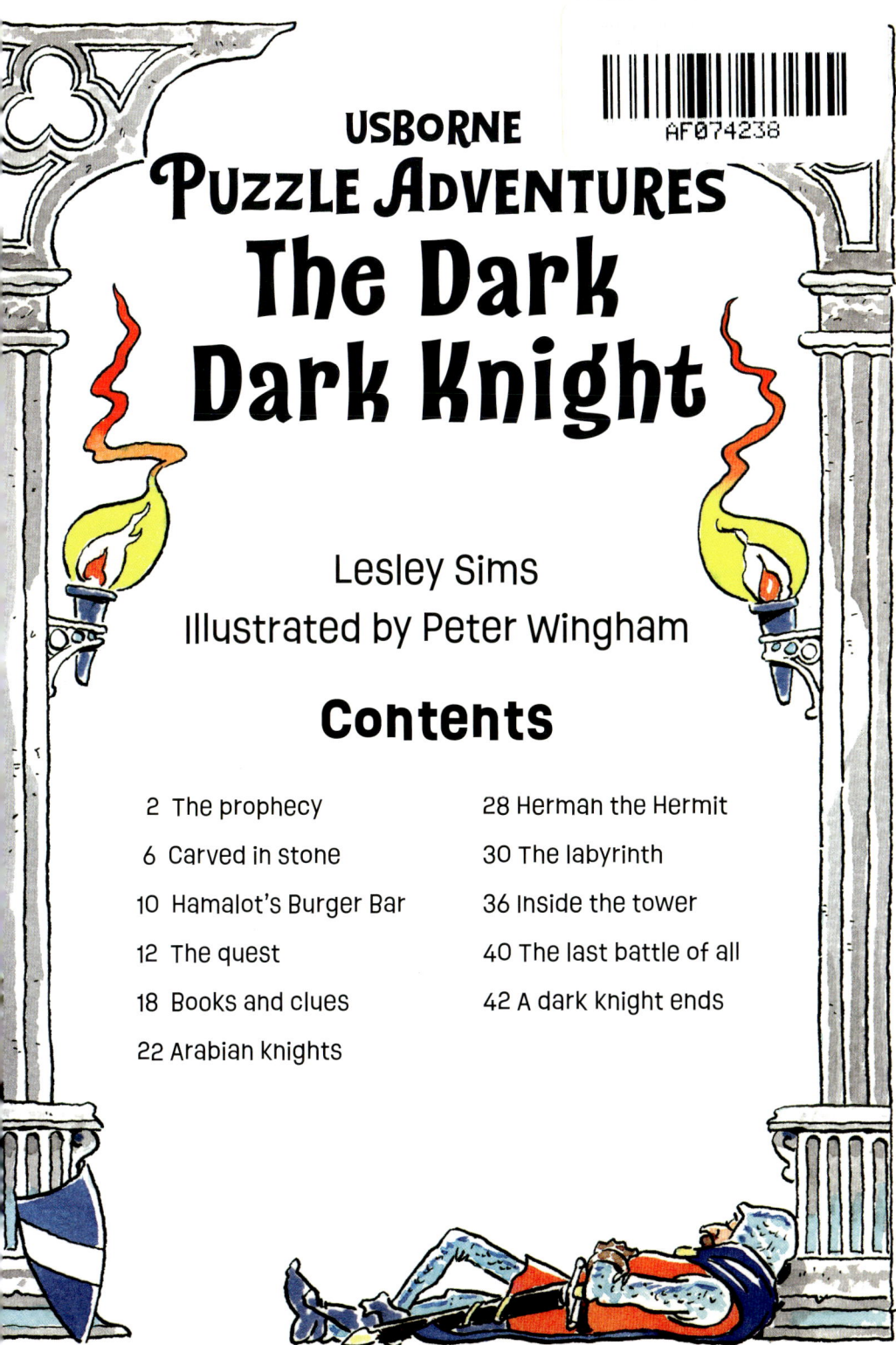

The prophecy

Welcome. I am Nerlym the Enchanter. The tale you are about to read began many centuries ago in the kingdom of Hamalot. Watch it unfold in the smoke from my fire...

Once, Hamalot was ruled by **Good King Stan**. He spent most of his time fighting off fiendish beasts.

The beasts were sent by the **Dark Dark Knight**, a villain no one had ever seen. He gave orders through an evil witch named **Nastina**.

Thurs 3 p.m.: Grand Battle between Good King Stan and the Dark Dark Knight!

The Dark Dark Knight grew stronger. So Stan agreed to a battle to decide the fate of the kingdom.

As the battle was about to begin, three of Stan's most loyal knights vanished...

...while King Stan was captured, and held by a spell in Nastina's **Tower of Desolation**.

Everyone was in despair. And so it continued for centuries. A dark cloud hung over Hamalot. But all was not lost, for there was a prophecy...

But I must let you find out what happened next. As the tale continues, our heroes will face lots of puzzles and brain-teasing problems. Join them to find the answers and unravel the mystery of the Dark Dark Knight.

Study the pictures to look out for vital clues and information. Sometimes you'll need to flick back through the book to find an answer.

Psst... there are **extra clues** on page 43, and you can check all the **answers** on pages 44-48.

Over two thousand years after King Stan was captured, two friends named Hallie and Martha were standing where the battle should have been fought... in Hallie's kitchen.

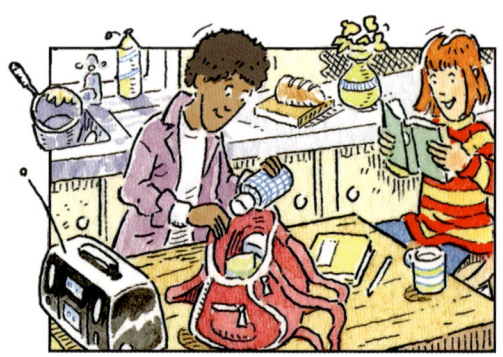

They were packing up a picnic for Yew Tree Forest, when the radio burst into life with a newsflash.

...very odd things are happening. All the books in the library have turned into bats and flown away. A gale has blown up from nowhere, and the town museum has been ransacked...

As they headed for the bus, a gust of wind blew a piece of paper straight into Hallie's hand.

On the bus, Hallie showed it to Martha. "It doesn't make any sense!" she said. "It isn't even addressed to anyone."

Just then the bus reached their stop, so Hallie shoved the note in her pocket.

The forest felt gloomier than usual as they headed to the picnic spot. But they must have taken a wrong turn. Finally, they had to admit they were completely lost.

"Is that a door?" asked Martha in surprise, spying something through the trees. "Oh... It's locked." A breeze rustled the leaves above them. "Key..." it seemed to say.

Can you see a key?

Carved in stone

The door creaked open to reveal a silent chapel, lit by a single candle. Before them was a vast stone tomb, bearing two strangely lifelike figures.

Hallie peered at the writing on the tomb's base. "This is a weird language," she muttered. "It's almost like a code…"

"Hey, Martha! Listen to this," she said, a little while later. But Martha had found a horn.

"WAIT!" shouted Hallie. She was too late. Martha blew it.

What does the writing on the tomb say?

The walls shook. Dust clouds filled the air. And then the two stone figures began to move. Martha and Hallie watched in stunned silence.

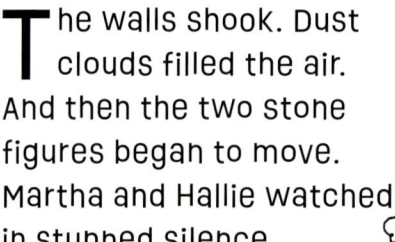

The stone knights, who weren't stone at all, stood up and brushed themselves down.

"Hey!" shouted one. "Where's the battle? We KLOTs have to defeat the villain. The entire kingdom is at stake!"

"B-battle?" repeated Hallie, still in shock.

"V-villain?" said Martha.

The other knight was reading the tombstone. "Uh-oh," he groaned. "Sir Roy, listen to this."

"Treachery, Sir Simon!" shouted Sir Roy. He stared at Hallie and Martha. "You look VERY odd," he declared, "but never mind that. We must go to the castle keep immediately!"

"Um, there's no castle near here," said Martha.

"Yes there is," Sir Roy insisted. "It's a magnificent sight. A river runs to the east. Northeast is the famous Awlup Hill. There's a monastery directly to the south of the castle keep and it's just inside the city walls. You can't miss it."

"Maybe there was a castle here once," said Hallie, fishing a map from her bag.

Where do you think the castle keep was?

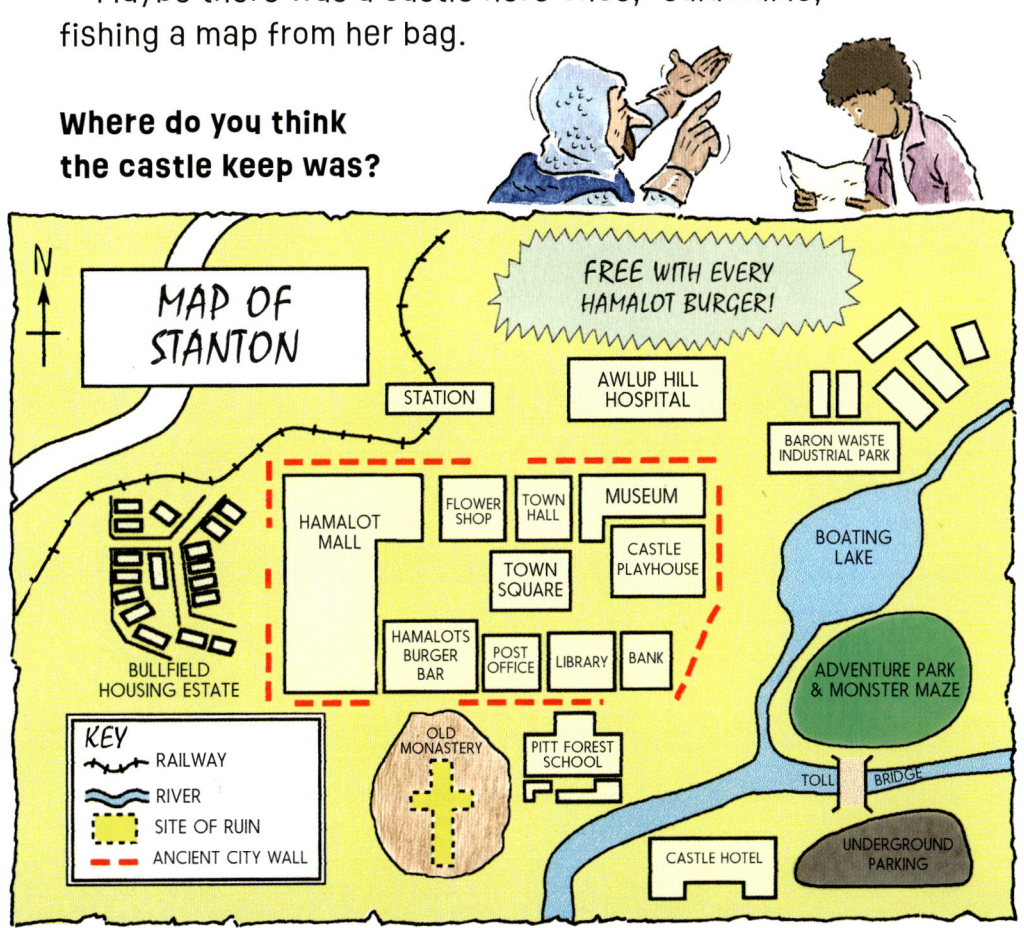

Hamalot's Burger Bar

Ten minutes later, they were at the site of the old castle keep, now Hamalot's Burger Bar. But the knights weren't interested in burgers. They wanted their king, Stan.

Just then, a man appeared and shouted in surprise. "Sir Roy! Sir Simon! What are you doing here?"

"Sir Percy?" exclaimed Sir Simon, the larger knight. "We've come to the castle keep, only... where is it?"

Martha and Hallie were more confused then ever. "Meet Sir Percy," said Sir Simon. "Knight Watchman and Keeper of Time."

"Shh! I'm here undercover," hissed Sir Percy. "And you two have to go back at once. Just after you vanished, the king was captured. Use my Timedial," he added, handing a bemused Sir Roy a pocket sundial.

"Say when and where you want to go, turn the pointer to the T factor and press the button. You can only go back, not forward, and it will only work twice. Good luck!"

"Hamalot Castle, just after the battle," gabbled Sir Roy, setting the pointer to eight. He hit the button and the Timedial flew through the air.

Hallie caught the Timedial with a worried frown. "No, not eight!" she cried, just as a brilliant white light blinded their eyes.

Is eight the right number?

To find the T factor: If there are 1 or 2 people going back, multiply the number going back by 9. If there are 3-6 people going back, multiply the number going back by 3. Then subtract one third. Transports maximum of 6 people!

The quest

In a flash, the burger bar vanished. Hallie and Martha were in a dazzlingly blue room, along with Sir Simon and Sir Roy. An old man with a long, white beard beckoned to them.

"I am Nerlym the Enchanter," he declared. "Welcome to Hamalot Castle, brave Halo and the Martyr."

"Brave Halo and WHO?" said Martha. "I think you're confusing us with someone else."

Nerlym shook his head. "We've been expecting you."

"This is the Blue Briefing Room," he went on. "We're planning your quest to rescue King Stan. Let me explain..."

By the end of his tale, the girls were horrified. Somehow, they had gone back in time. Now, they had to go on some quest. Worst of all, they couldn't go home until they had.

"The details of the quest are on this scroll," said Nerlym. "But it's in ancient Chivalric." It looked like an easy code. **Can you decipher the message?**

TheQric uestric forKric ingSric tanric

BraveHa lo,Ma rtyrric, heresric yourric Quesric t:tofric reeNric asti na'scric aptu redgric uestric. Firsric t,you mustric findric twocric hainric mailric vestric s,astric arryric sworric dandric shie lds.Tric hensric eekwric isemric onksric who'lric ltelric lyou more ofho wtorric eachric Nastric ina'sric doorric. Yourric shie ldswric illhric elpyric oucro sshe rflo oranric dthe nherric fate isse aledric.

Nerlym gave them the scroll and led them outside. "Just so you know, Nastina only has power over three things. Anything else is an illusion. Good luck!"

"What three things?" asked Hallie, but Nerlym had gone.

Martha shrugged. "I suppose we must find shields and this chain mail," she said, doubtfully. "Let's ask that gardener if he can help."

"Um, I think he's nibbling leaves," said Hallie.

"You need Sir John, the swordsmith. Seee Sirrr Johhhhn," the gardener bleated. Before their shocked gazes, he turned into a goat and butted Hallie onto a different path.

"Was he a goat?" Hallie said, bewildered. Martha giggled.

"Can I help you?" called out a knight in front of a hut.

"Are you Sir John?" asked Hallie. "The, um, gardener told us to see you."

"Barry the Weregoat?" said Sir John, smiling. "He's harmless. Come on in."

Sir John found them chain mail tunics, and shields with odd messages on the backs.

"Swords are trickier," he said. "They're handmade and there's a waiting list." He pointed to a heap of old metal on the floor. "But you should find something there."

Can you see which four pieces fit together to make a sword?

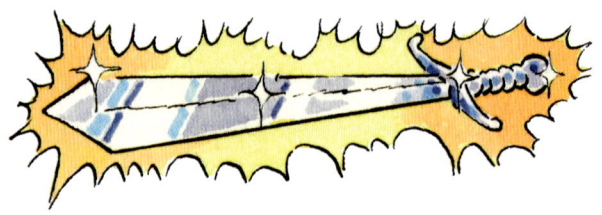

No sooner had Hallie put the last piece of sword in place than it sprang together, glowing like new. "Next on the list, find wise monks," said Martha, checking the scroll.

As luck would have it, there in the distance were two. "We can follow them," said Martha, grinning. "This is easy!"
At last they reached a monastery. "We're on a quest," Hallie explained to a monk at the door. "Can you help?"

LIBRARY ENTRANCE
TO PASS, FIRST PASS
THE ENTRANCE TEST

The monk sent them to the library, where a second monk pointed to a sign over the door. "But—" Martha began.
The monk frowned and gave them a parchment and quill.

"A test?" Martha hissed to Hallie. "It's like school!"

"It's okay, it's just a word search and a puzzle," Hallie whispered back.

Can you solve the puzzles?

Brother Ben's Brainteasers

Find the fiends!

D	W	B	H	A	G	I	L
E	R	E	T	S	N	O	M
R	D	A	F	R	T	G	N
I	W	S	G	N	O	I	T
P	A	T	A	O	L	L	C
M	R	I	G	B	N	V	L
A	G	R	O	F	H	A	B
V	E	G	K	O	O	P	S

Can you strike out all ten fiends hidden in the grid? (They are listed around the edge of the parchment.)

HAG BEAST VAMPIRE DRAGON MONSTER GIANT OGRE GOBLIN SPOOK TROLL

Monk-y Puzzle

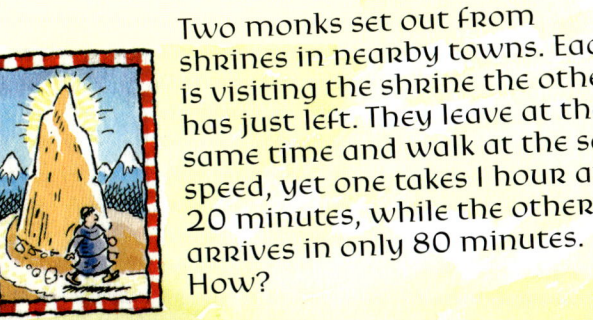

Two monks set out from shrines in nearby towns. Each is visiting the shrine the other has just left. They leave at the same time and walk at the same speed, yet one takes 1 hour and 20 minutes, while the other arrives in only 80 minutes. How?

Books and clues

With a stern, "Keep quiet!" they were let into the library. Rows of monks sat in silence, copying manuscripts. A tall monk came over to them.

"We need to know how to find Nastina's Tower," Martha murmured.

Hallie rustled the scroll.

"Sshhh!" ordered several monks, all waving quills.

The tall monk grabbed an old book and handed it to Martha, who put it on a nearby table. A great jumble of papers and dried flowers fell out.

"How does this help?" Martha mouthed to Hallie. But as they read all the information, they quickly realized what to do next.

Where should they go first?

CURIOUS CHARACTERS OF OUR TIME
(Free with a bushel of oats)
No. 27 Herman the Hermit

Herman lives at the edge of the Barren Wastes. He became a hermit one wet Thursday, when the other villagers banished him for talking too much. He is a famous water diviner. In his spare time, he carves pipes from rushes which grow in the boggy marshes of the Barren Wastes.

CLOISTERS CHRONICLE

KING KIDNAPPED!
by Brother Dan

Good King Stan has been the victim of a terrible trick and is now being held prisoner in the grim Tower of Desolation.

As the Great Battle was about to begin, three loyal KLOTs were spirited away and Stan was grabbed by Nastina's Nasties.

Each day, the Dark Dark Knight's powers grow stronger...

Learn to read & write in 5 days! For further details, write to The Monastery.

EARL GREY OF BERGAMOT CASTLE:
importer of the finest spices and leaves from Araby

DID YOU KNOW?
The pipes made by Herman have magical powers. They can even hypnotize the ferocious dragon, Phaal.

The Wandring Minstrels
In concert at the Castle Inn. Doors open at 4 p.m.

To release a knight from an evil enchantment, call his name three times.

Herman won't accept money for his pipes, but he will exchange one for the rare Hytee leaves from Araby.

The Towers of Hamalot
The Tower of Desolation

This tower sits in the Barren Wastes and is home to the evil Nastina. Though everyone knows it exists, no one knows what it looks like as it is usually invisible.

The tower is defended by three obstacles. Each one must be overcome before the next one appears.

The door to the tower is blocked by **Silverkeys the Guardian**.

Artist's impression of the tower

To reach **Silverkeys** you must get past the **Three Crones**, who are guarded by the ferocious dragon, **Phaal**.

Phaal and the Three Crones

Phaal lives in a devious labyrinth. He is immortal, but can be hypnotized. Until he's defeated, the **crones** are hidden.

19

First, they had to visit Earl Grey, but by now it was dark so they stayed overnight with the monks.

They set off at sunrise. Before long, Martha was moaning. "My feet hurt! I wish we had a horse." No sooner had she spoken, than one appeared.

"Weird!" cried Martha, leaping astride the huge beast and hauling up Hallie behind her.

The horse reared up and then galloped off so quickly it was all they could do to cling on. Suddenly, it stopped — so abruptly, Martha and Hallie went flying over its head and landed in a deep pit.

"Gotcha!" bellowed a voice. "Ha! New servants for me cookings and cleanings. Stays there till I needs you."

Hallie stood up slowly. "Nothing broken," she said, shakily. "Who IS he?" she added to Martha. "Looks like he escaped from a fairy tale."

Martha didn't hear. She was reading a stone slab propped against the pit wall. "I gain Mac spells Abracadabra?"

"Ha! Them's me riddles!" said the creature. "If you gets them right, I mights let you go..."

Martha grinned. "They're just anagrams!" She and Hallie reeled off the answers.

"...then again, I mights NOT," said the creature firmly.

"I wish I'd never jumped on that horse," said Martha.

"That's it!" said Hallie. When she fell, she had landed on something hard in her pocket. "We can easily get out."

What is Hallie's escape plan?

With the leaves safely in Hallie's pocket, they set out again. After a while, they reached a fork in the track. "Which way now?" said Hallie.

Martha spotted a figure up ahead. "Let's ask him," she began, but Hallie stopped her.
"That shield on his tunic — it's the same as on the Dark Dark Knight's note! I wonder what he's up to..."

The man slipped between two rocks and down a flight of stone steps. Silently, they followed.

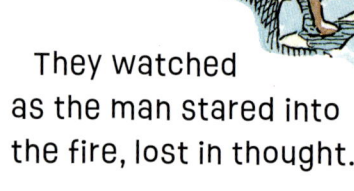

They watched as the man stared into the fire, lost in thought.

24

He took out a letter, read it and then tore it in four, dropping the pieces by the fire. With a grunt, he hurried from the room.

Martha and Hallie dashed in and picked up the letter.

"It's from the Dark Dark Knight!" gasped Martha. "If we can put it together, we might learn more about him."

What does the letter say?

"That villain!" said Hallie. "We must find Herman, now!" Martha pulled her back. "Wait! That servant was going to the Tower. We'll be quicker if we simply follow him."

The steps led to a tunnel. Hallie scrambled along, behind Martha, spotting some paper on the ground. Had Martha dropped it? Hallie quickly put it in her pocket.

Outside the tunnel was a river with a handy bridge. They were about to cross it when—

"This is a troll toll bridge," snarled a creature, blocking their way. "I'm the troll. Pay me a toll... or fight my knight!"

The troll let out a piercing whistle, and a dazed knight staggered up. He was huge and silent and his eyes seemed glazed over.

Gripping Hallie's shoulder, he led her to a fierce horse and gave her a lance.
"But I can't fight. I'm not a knight!" she protested.

Martha watched in horror. Why was a knight in league with a horrible warty troll?

With a start, she realized he was a KLOT. And it looked as though he was enchanted. She'd read in the library that calling his name three times would break the spell. But what was his name?

Do you know?

Herman the Hermit

Martha called his name, and Sir Gavin awoke. While he chased after the troll, Martha and Hallie raced over the bridge.

As they left the bridge, a mist came out of nowhere. It wrapped itself around them until they couldn't see a thing.

"Ow!"

"Martha, are you okay?"

"Hallie, was that you?"

"Be careful!" complained a voice. "I'm divining."

The mist began to clear, and they saw the owner of the voice. "I'm Herman," he said, with a little bow.

It was Herman the Hermit, the very person they needed. Martha told him about their quest, while Hallie handed over some slightly crushed leaves.

"For me? How kind," he said, leading them to his hut. He started hunting for a pipe, chattering to himself.

Hallie and Martha looked around. The hut was cramped and had an odd, damp smell.

"Aha!" Herman said at last, waving a pipe and some music.

"The problem," he added, "is that my pipes only hypnotize the dragon if you can find him. I've spent years hunting. I even bought this music, guaranteed to lead me to him. But when I played it, nothing happened..."

"I don't think it *is* music," said Hallie, looking at it closely. "I think it's coded directions made to look like music."
What are the directions?

The labyrinth

The directions led from a purple rock to a red one. Hallie sat on it with a bump, and some paper fell from her pocket. "Oh, you dropped those in the tunnel," she said as Martha read them. But they weren't Martha's.

> Fred – you must feed Phaal. If I leave the Tower, my hold over Stan is weakened.
> Go to the Red Rock and chant this rhyme, "Mighty Nastina, she who commands serpents, stone and steel, now bids you answer her demand: the dragon's lair reveal!"
> You will find yourself where I have marked "X" on the plan.
> Nastina

"It's a note from Nastina," said Martha. She recited the rhyme and then... Walls suddenly rose up around them and they were in the bottom corner of the labyrinth.

"Now for Phaal," Hallie said and gulped.

Can you find a way to Phaal in the middle of the labyrinth?

At the top of the steps leading to the heart of the maze, they paused. Then, taking a breath, they went down together... **ROOOOOAAARRRHHH!** ...and leaped back in terror, as a sheet of flame shot out at them.

"Quick! The pipe!" croaked Martha. Hallie's mouth was dry, but she stuck in the pipe and blew. A few quavery notes hovered on the air. They sounded terrible.

Phaal snarled. Martha shut her eyes. But Hallie played some more, gently moving the pipe from side to side. Phaal followed the pipe... left... right... left...

His eyes flickered and closed. Slowly, he sank down onto a huge pile of treasure and let out a rumbling snore.

Now they could see a door leading outside. But as they tried to leave, a crone blocked the exit.

"I cannot see without my glasses. Find them and I'll give you passes," she cackled.

A second crone joined her. "What's that you say? You'll have to shout. Find my megaphone. I'll let you out."

"Wiffout my teef, I cannot chew. If I faint from hunger, you won't get frew," gabbled a third.

Martha smiled. "And if we find your glasses, megaphone and false teeth, you'll let us out?" The third crone nodded.
Hallie looked at the sleeping dragon. "Hope he's not lying on them! We'll have to find them before he wakes up."

Can you see the missing things?

The crones grasped their things with cries of glee, and Hallie and Martha slipped through the exit.

A solid wall, shrouded in mist, blocked their way. Then a door studded with spikes appeared. Hallie touched the door cautiously. "It feels real," she said. "Let's go in."

Inside was a courtyard, paved like a chess board, and opposite them at last — the Tower of Desolation.

A goblin with jingling keys on his belt strode up to them.

"So you got past Phaal and the crones," he said with a sneer. "You won't defeat me! There's only one way to the tower. Step on the wrong stone at the wrong time, and..."

He threw a twig onto a square. With a fizzzzz, it dissolved into nothingness.

"Only the white squares with flags are always safe," he added. He pointed to a sundial. "Reach the door by twelve and I'll unlock it. If not, you'll be thrown in the dungeons."

Hallie gasped. The shadow was almost at twelve already. Then a line from the scroll came to her.
Your shields will help you cross her floor...
"The shields show the way!" she told Martha. "The lines on mine show the direction. The symbols on yours show how many squares. My first line is green and points north. You have two green trees, so we go two squares north."

Can you find the safe way to the door?

Inside the tower

The tower door slammed shut behind them. Hallie and Martha looked around. A spiral staircase filled the small hallway.

"Here we go," said Martha and began to climb.

Darkened rooms led off the stairs. They peered around half-closed doors, each time terrified that one would open on Nastina.

Finally, they found a bright room with a smiling knight. Was this King Stan?

Hallie was uneasy. It felt unreal. Martha was going in, so Hallie grabbed her.

"Wait!" she said. As she spoke, the knight and the room vanished. They were left teetering on the brink of a gaping hole. Hallie hauled Martha back — just in time.

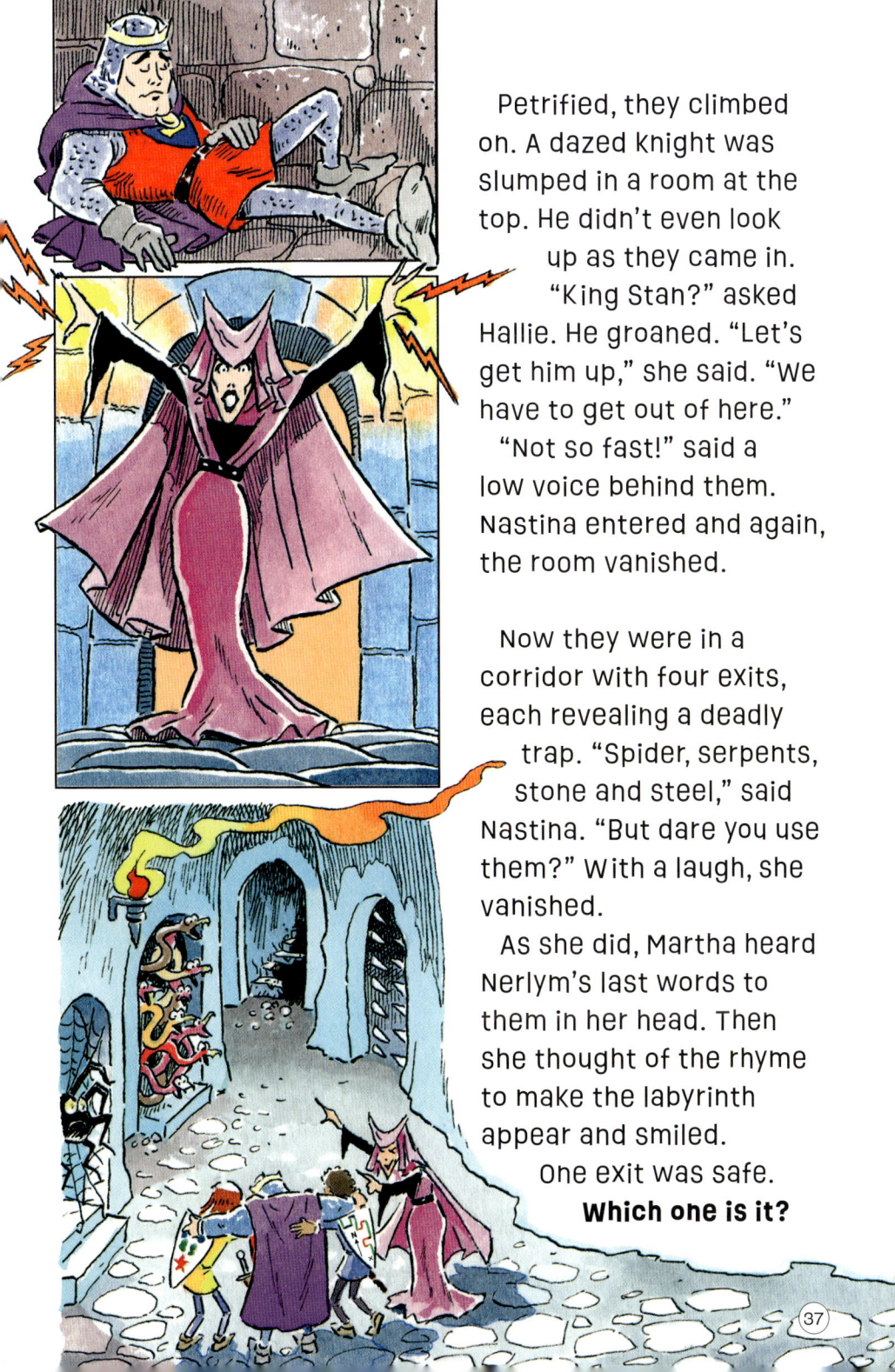

Petrified, they climbed on. A dazed knight was slumped in a room at the top. He didn't even look up as they came in.

"King Stan?" asked Hallie. He groaned. "Let's get him up," she said. "We have to get out of here."

"Not so fast!" said a low voice behind them. Nastina entered and again, the room vanished.

Now they were in a corridor with four exits, each revealing a deadly trap. "Spider, serpents, stone and steel," said Nastina. "But dare you use them?" With a laugh, she vanished.

As she did, Martha heard Nerlym's last words to them in her head. Then she thought of the rhyme to make the labyrinth appear and smiled.

One exit was safe. **Which one is it?**

As Hallie stepped into the web, it vanished. They heaved the dazed king into the fresh air, where he quickly revived.

"Where am I? Who are YOU?" he asked, looking bemused.

"No time to explain," Hallie panted. "We must get to Hamalot NOW!"

"We'll be there in a trice," said King Stan, calling out for Nerlym. And, quicker than a blink, they were.

"Sire! Heroines!" said Nerlym. "I'd almost given up hope. And I know the Dark Dark Knight is plotting something..."

"He wants to be invincible," said Martha, "using some goblet. And I've seen it somewhere. But where?"

"We must find it first," declared King Stan. "Gather the KLOTs!"

"They're all over the castle," said Nerlym. "It will take a while to find them."

The knights were enjoying a free afternoon, but finally nearly all of them were gathered in the Great Hall.

"We're leaving now to find a goblet and defeat the Dark Dark Knight," King Stan shouted, amid cheers. "Um, where ARE we going?" All at once, Martha knew where she had seen the goblet before. **Where was the Moon Goblet?**

The last battle of all

Nerlym clicked his fingers. Instantly, the castle became the burger bar, but the Moon Goblet had gone.

"Quick! Outside by the fountain," said Hallie. They tore out to see the Dark Dark Knight frantically scooping up water.

"STOP!" yelled King Stan. He knocked the goblet to the ground and a desperate duel began. With a lucky stroke, the Dark Dark Knight flicked Stan's sword from his hand.

Martha and Hallie quickly handed the king their sword.

King Stan pinned down the villain, trying to remove his helmet and scratching his face in the struggle. Then...

...clouds of thick, black smoke surrounded them. When the smoke cleared, the Dark Dark Knight had gone.

The KLOTs looked horrified. "He escaped!" groaned the king. Hallie and Martha smiled. He was no longer the Dark Dark Knight, but he hadn't gone far. They knew where he was.

Do you?

A dark knight ends

"It's him!" Hallie said, pointing to Sir Jack Upall.

"Nonsense!" said King Stan.

"We can prove it," Martha insisted. "The Dark Dark Knight wrote a letter telling his servant about us. Only Nerlym and the KLOTs knew we'd arrived."

"When we left the castle, there was a knight missing," added Hallie. "But now all the KLOTs are here."

"Look at his cheek," said Martha. "Only just grazed in the duel."

"Grab him!" ordered King Stan. He bowed. "Thank you for all your help. Now we must return to our own time before any more harm is done."

He called for Nerlym and Hallie and Martha were alone.

"Let's go home," said Martha after a few seconds. "I want to check my history book — and read about King Stan's glorious rescue by Brave Halo and the Martyr!"

Clues

Pages 4-5
Keys don't grow on trees...
...do they?

Pages 6-7
Each word has been reversed, with a letter added in front.

Pages 8-9
Some places may have changed.

Pages 10-11
Only two people should be going back — Sir Simon and Sir Roy.

Pages 12-13
Chivalric breaks up words into groups and adds **ric** to all groups not ending in a vowel.

Pages 14-15
There are pieces for more than one sword in the pile.

Pages 16-17
Study the word puzzle closely. How many minutes are in 1 hour and 20 minutes?

Pages 18-19
Start at the Tower of Desolation and work back. To enter, Hallie and Martha must defeat Silverkeys the Guardian. How do they reach him?

Pages 20-21
What happens on page 11?

Pages 22-23
Using what you know, you can fill in the gaps.

Pages 24-25
Trace the pieces and fit them together.

Pages 26-27
A KLOT was missing when they arrived. Check the shields on page 12.

Pages 28-29
The alphabet chant in the library gives each note a letter.

Pages 30-31
Watch out for blind alleys.

Pages 32-33
Search the treasure carefully.

Pages 34-35
A red line = 1 square

Pages 36-37
What does the rhyme on page 30 say Nastina has power over?

Pages 38-39
Martha saw the Moon Goblet before they went back in time.

Pages 40-41
The Dark Dark Knight has gone — but who is the knight who has just arrived?

Answers

Pages 4-5
The key is circled.

Pages 6-7
Each word has been written backwards and begins with an extra letter. Decoded, the inscription reads:

HERE, UNDER MY SPELL, LIE TWO MOST PUNY KNIGHTS, SIR SIMON AND SIR ROY. IN THIS CHAPEL THEY SHALL SLEEP FOREVER, UNLESS SOMEONE DECIPHERS MY MESSAGE AND WAKES THEM. THE HORN OF AWAKENING WILL ROUSE THEM. BLOW IT... IF YOU DARE. NASTINA AD20

The extra letters also make a sentence:
HEED MY WARNING. DO NOT MEDDLE OR YOU WILL REGRET IT! HA

Pages 8-9
If you match the descriptions of the old landmarks to the places shown on the modern map, you will see Hamalot's Burger Bar stands on the site of the castle keep. The Awlup Hill is now the Awlup Hill Hospital.

Pages 10-11
The right number was twelve. The correct sum is:
2 (two knights) x 9 = 18 - 6 (one third of 18) = **12**.
Sir Roy multiplied 4 x 3 = 12 - 4 (one third of 12) = 8 and took Hallie and Martha back with him and Sir Simon.

Pages 12-13
Decoded, the message reads: ***The Quest for King Stan***

Brave Halo, Martyr, here's your Quest: to free Nastina's captured guest. First, you must find two chain mail vests, a starry sword and shields. Then seek wise monks who'll tell you more of how to reach Nastina's door. Your shields will help you cross her floor and then her fate is sealed.

Pages 14-15
The pieces they need have been circled.

The sword fits together like this:

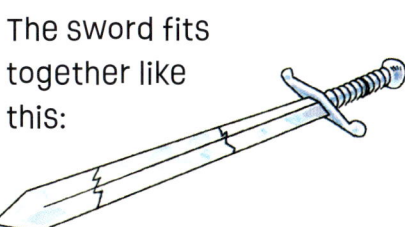

Pages 16-17
Find the fiends

Monk-y Puzzle
1 hour (60 minutes) and 20 minutes is the same as 80 minutes.

Pages 18-19
The old book about the Towers of Hamalot says to enter the Tower of Desolation, Hallie and Martha must first defeat Silverkeys the Guardian.

To reach Silverkeys, they must get past the Three Crones — and to reach the Three Crones they must find and defeat the dragon, Phaal.

The Cloisters Chronicle tells them that Phaal can be hypnotized with one of Herman's pipes, and a scrap of paper says that Herman will swap a pipe for Hytee leaves from Araby.

The Cloisters Chronicle also has an advertisement for Earl Grey, who imports spices and leaves from Araby, so Bergamot Castle is where they should start.

Pages 20-21

Hallie still has Sir Percy's Timedial. She caught it on page 11. Her plan is to go back in time to just before they saw the horse, then ignore it.

The three anagrams are **magician**, **adventure** and **chocolate**.

Pages 22-23

Sir Nutmeg wears blue, and the person in blue brought perfume, so Sir Nutmeg has the perfume.

Lord Sage brought gems and they were brought by the person in green, so Lord Sage wears green.

Duke Turmeric brought silks. He must wear red because Prince Clove wears yellow.

So Prince Clove, in yellow, has the Hytee leaves.

Pages 24-25

When the letter is pieced together, this is what it says:

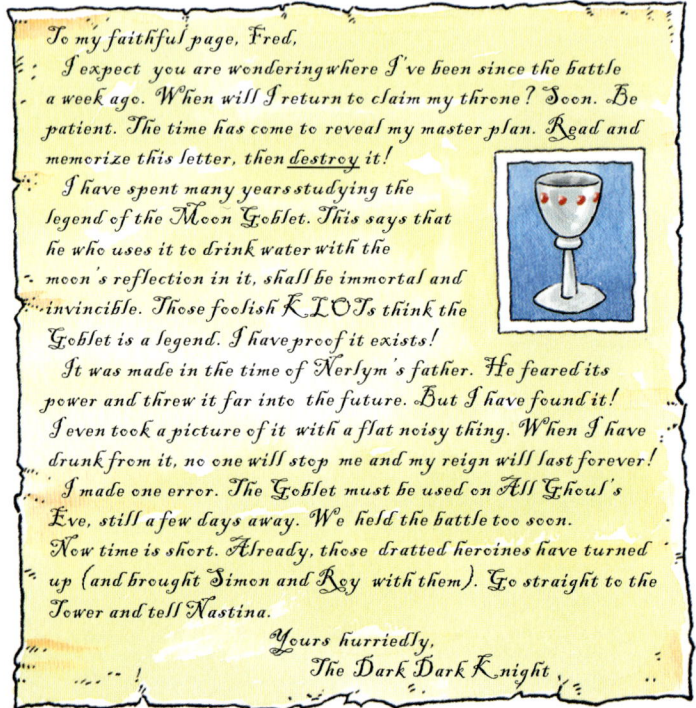

To my faithful page, Fred,

I expect you are wondering where I've been since the battle a week ago. When will I return to claim my throne? Soon. Be patient. The time has come to reveal my master plan. Read and memorize this letter, then <u>destroy</u> it!

I have spent many years studying the legend of the Moon Goblet. This says that he who uses it to drink water with the moon's reflection in it, shall be immortal and invincible. Those foolish KLOTs think the Goblet is a legend. I have proof it exists!

It was made in the time of Nerlym's father. He feared its power and threw it far into the future. But I have found it! I even took a picture of it with a flat noisy thing. When I have drunk from it, no one will stop me and my reign will last forever!

I made one error. The Goblet must be used on All Ghoul's Eve, still a few days away. We held the battle too soon.

Now time is short. Already, those dratted heroines have turned up (and brought Simon and Roy with them). Go straight to the Tower and tell Nastina.

Yours hurriedly,
The Dark Dark Knight

Pages 26-27
The knight is Sir Gavin Goode. He was enchanted by Nastina and given to the troll.

Pages 28-29
The music can be decoded using Brother Gregory's Alphabet Chant, shown in the library on pages 18-19.
If you match the notes from there with the ones on Herman's music, a message is revealed.
Go nine paces N(orth) and ten paces E(ast).

Pages 30-31
Their route through the labyrinth is shown in blue.

Pages 32-33
The three missing things have been circled in pink.

Pages 34-35
This is their route:

Pages 36-37

The spider doorway is the exit they must take.
On page 14, Nerlym told Martha and Hallie that Nastina only had power over three things.
The rhyme to make the labyrinth appear (page 30) tells you the three things are serpents, stone and steel. Three of the doorways show serpents, steel spikes and stone steps. Nerlym said anything else was an illusion, so Martha realizes that the spider and its web are not really there.

Pages 38-39

The Moon Goblet is on page 11, in Hamalot's Burger Bar, being used to hold straws.

Pages 40-41

The Dark Dark Knight has been circled: he's Sir Jack Upall, who has just appeared from nowhere.
He was seen in the castle on page 12, but not since. When Nerlym collected all the knights on page 39, he was the only knight who wasn't there.

Series editors: Lesley Sims and Gaby Waters
Designed by Laura Nelson Norris and Lucy Smith
Digital imaging: John Russell

This edition first published in 2025 by Usborne Publishing Limited, 83-85 Saffron Hill, London EC1N 8RT, United Kingdom. usborne.com Copyright © 2025, 2005, 1995 Usborne Publishing Limited. The name Usborne and the Balloon logo are registered trade marks of Usborne Publishing Limited. All rights reserved. No part of this publication may be reproduced or used in any manner for the purpose of training artificial intelligence technologies or systems (including for text or data mining), stored in retrieval systems or transmitted in any form or by any means without prior permission of the publisher. UE